Series 522

JESUS CALLS HIS DISCIPLES

by LUCY DIAMOND
with illustrations
by KENNETH INNS

Ladybird Books Ltd Loughborough

JESUS CALLS HIS DISCIPLES

This story begins when there was trouble and unrest among the Jews. They hated their Roman conquerors, and the whole nation longed for, and anxiously awaited, the coming of the One Who should be its Saviour.

Many expected that this promised Messiah would free them from the power of Rome, and Himself rule in Jerusalem.

They never dreamed that for nearly thirty years He had been living in a humble home in Nazareth of Galilee, and working as a village carpenter.

Then a man was sent from God, whose name was John. He came into the wilderness of Judæa, round about Jordan, preaching and saying " The kingdom of Heaven is at hand. Be sorry for your sins, and make ready for the coming of the Lord."

Soon crowds went out from Jerusalem to listen to John's teaching.

This unknown preacher was a strange figure in his rough dress of camel's hair fastened with a leather girdle. He lived in the wilderness, and fed on locusts—a sweet bean—and wild honey. Some among the crowd who heard how fearlessly he rebuked wrong doing, even in the rich and great, wondered if he could be the prophet Elijah come back with a message for God's people.

The multitudes were roused by John's stern words. Many were ashamed to remember how often they had forgotten God and broken His laws.

" What must we do ? " they asked him.

" Repent," was the answer. " Make amends for your wrong doing. Then I will baptize you."

After that people came in hundreds, and John baptized them in the River Jordan.

So he became known over all the countryside as John the Baptist.

John did not stay always in the wilderness of Judæa. Slowly he made his way northwards, keeping to the wild, hilly country beyond Jordan, and preaching and baptizing as he went.

At last he reached Bethabara, a place close by one of the best known fords in Jordan. Here the Baptist was only about twenty miles from Nazareth, and within reach of the villages and towns of Galilee. He could preach to travellers coming and going across the river.

Even as far north as Bethabara everyone had heard of John. It was while he was preaching there that Jesus came from Nazareth to be baptized.

And, by a sign from heaven, John knew that this was the Saviour Whose coming he had been sent to proclaim.

But Jesus was not yet ready to begin His ministry.

The chief priests and rulers in Jerusalem soon heard of this wonderful prophet, and grew anxious. Who could this man be who preached and baptized in the Name of the God of Israel?

They sent messengers to John at Bethabara, asking " Who are you ? Are you the Messiah—the Christ ? "

" No," John answered, " I am only a voice proclaiming His coming. My work is nearly done, for now He is here."

The Baptist then told them how, weeks before, Jesus of Nazareth had come to him to be baptized.

" And as He came from the water," John went on, " the heavens opened, and I saw the Holy Spirit in the form of a dove come down and rest upon Him. I knew by that sign that this was the Son of God—the promised Messiah."

Among the crowds of Galileans who crossed the Jordan to hear John preach were fishermen from Bethsaida and Capernaum, towns by the Sea of Galilee. They were all close friends—James and John, the sons of Zebedee, Simon and Andrew, two brothers, and Philip, their neighbour.

These young men were so thrilled by the teaching of the Baptist, that they lingered day after day at Bethabara. They became John's disciples, to learn all they could about the Messiah, the Saviour for Whom he had prepared the way.

They were there when the messengers came, and listened eagerly, especially as they asked their last question :

" Where can we find Him? "

But John could not tell them. After His baptism Jesus had gone alone into the wilderness. There for forty days He fasted and prayed, and conquered the devil who tempted Him.

The messengers went back to Jerusalem, but all those who heard John's words were startled. Could this amazing thing be true ? Had the Messiah really come, and if so, where was He ?

Even the Baptist did not know.

But the very next morning Jesus returned from the wilderness, and John saw Him in the distance.

" Behold," he cried joyfully to the crowd, " behold the Lamb of God, which taketh away the sin of the world. He is the One of Whom I have spoken. He is mightier than I. I am not worthy even to unloose the latchet of His shoes. He will teach you about the Kingdom of Heaven, and baptize you with the Holy Spirit."

The people turned quickly to look, but they only saw dimly a far off figure, for Jesus had passed on.

The next day the Baptist was talking to two of his disciples, Andrew and John, the son of Zebedee, when again in the distance he saw Jesus walking.

" Look! " he said to them, " There is the Lamb of God—the Christ ! "

At once the two left John, and hurried after the Man he had pointed out.

The prophet's eyes must have been very wistful as he watched them go. He knew that they would not return to him. Yet humbly and unselfishly he rejoiced, because the Saviour he had so faithfully proclaimed had come at last.

The two friends almost ran in their eagerness, but suddenly the One they were following turned and waited for them.

Then they saw His face—and to his astonishment John realised that the Messiah was his own cousin—Jesus of Nazareth !

" What are you seeking ? " Jesus asked as the two came up to Him.

" Rabbi, Master," Andrew answered breathlessly, " where are you staying ? "

Jesus said, " Come and see."

So John and Andrew followed as the Master led them to His lodging. How glad they were when He invited them to stay with Him all that day !

Andrew longed to spread the news everywhere that the promised Saviour had come, but first he hurried to find his own brother Simon.

" Come quickly," he said to him, " we have found the Messiah, the Christ ! "

He brought him to Jesus.

Jesus looked at him with a welcoming smile.

" You are Simon the son of Jonas," He said. " You shall now be called Peter—the Rock."

Then Simon Peter joined the little group, and all through that happy day Jesus talked with them till evening.

Early next morning Jesus started on His way back to Galilee. John, Andrew and Peter went with Him, and probably John's brother James had now joined them. They were going towards Cana, a town about twenty miles from Bethabara, through which one passed to reach the Sea of Galilee. Jesus had been invited to a wedding there.

As they went, Andrew and Peter, who were walking in front, saw Philip their friend from Bethsaida. They hurried on to tell him what had happened.

Philip was just as excited as they were to hear that James' and John's cousin, Jesus of Nazareth, was really the Messiah, so Andrew and Peter eagerly led him to their newly-found Master.

Jesus spoke kindly as the three stood before Him.

" Philip," He said, " Follow Me."

And unhesitatingly Philip answered, " Master, I will."

It was a long journey on foot from Bethabara to Cana, but the miles seemed short, and time passed quickly as they talked with Jesus by the way.

At last they drew near to Cana. Philip had a friend there.

This was Nathanael, whose surname was Bartholomew.

He was a man well known in Cana, a good citizen and a devout Jew.

Nathanael lived in a white house at the foot of a hill. It had a pleasant garden, and in one corner of it a fig tree which, with its wide spreading branches, made a patch of cool shade.

This tree was the most treasured thing in Nathanael's garden. Every morning he spent an hour studying and praying in its friendly shade. Then he was doing as pious Jews had done through the centuries—worshipping God beneath his own fig tree.

As the little party of travellers neared Cana, Philip ran on before the others. He was eager to find his friend.

When he came to Nathanael's house, he found him sitting under his fig tree studying the scriptures.

He hurried up to him.

" Listen," he cried. " I have wonderful news! We have found the Messiah—the Saviour of Whom Moses and the prophets have spoken. He is Jesus of Nazareth."

Now Nathanael was a man of high standing, well learned in the Law and the prophets.

He was rather scornful.

" Nazareth!" he said. "A poor country village like that! Can any good thing come out of Nazareth ? "

Philip did not argue. Very simply he answered, " Come and see."

And he hastened to bring his friend to the One of Whom he had been telling.

Jesus saw Nathanael coming and spoke of him to the others.

" Look," He said, " here is an Israelite who is indeed straightforward and true."

Nathanael heard what Jesus said. He was surprised. He was sure he had never seen this Teacher before.

" How can you know me ? " he asked.

Jesus smiled as He answered, " I do know you Nathanael. Before Philip called you, when you were under the fig tree, I saw you."

Then indeed Nathanael believed.

He stood humbly before this Man from the despised village of Nazareth.

" Rabbi," he cried, " You are the Son of God. You are the King of Israel."

Jesus looked kindly at Philip's friend as He replied:

" O Nathanael, is it because I said I saw you under the fig tree that you believe ? I tell you, you shall see greater things than these."

Nathanael joined the others and they all went into Cana—six men who were so certain that Jesus was the Messiah that they were ready to follow Him anywhere.

But not yet were they called to give up everything to be His disciples.

Next day they were all at the wedding feast when the wine ran short, and Jesus turned water into wine so that the feast might end happily.

That was the first sign of the power of their Master. They realised His glory, and more firmly than ever they believed in Him.

Afterwards they returned to their own homes.

But some time passed before Jesus returned to Nazareth. Then at last in the synagogue there He told the people He was the Messiah.

They would not believe Him, and in furious anger drove Him from their village.

As the people of Nazareth would not receive Him, Jesus went to Capernaum, a busy town by the Sea of Galilee which for nearly three years was to be the centre of His ministry. There one morning He walked along the shore to where the fishermen were busy at their work.

He found Simon Peter and Andrew. The brothers were in their boat casting a net into the sea.

How glad they were to see their Master again !

But Jesus had not come just to talk to them. Now He had begun His ministry, He needed these disciples who already loved and trusted Him.

He beckoned to them.

" Come," He said. " Come after Me, and I will make you fishers of men."

At once the brothers left their nets and followed Him, ready to give up everything for their Lord.

A little farther along the shore they came to where another boat was moored. This belonged to Zebedee, the father of James and John.

Zebedee was a prosperous fish merchant. He had a fine, large ship, with hired servants to help him and his sons in their work.

That morning James and John were in the boat with their father and the servants. They were mending the nets torn by sharp stones under the water near the shore.

Suddenly John looked up, and there was Jesus standing with Andrew and Simon Peter on the shore. He was calling to them—

" Come after Me."

And straightway they left their father Zebedee in the boat with the hired servants, and followed Him.

So for James and John a new life began. They also were now to become fishers of men.

Now Jesus went about throughout Galilee, teaching in the synagogues, preaching and healing all kinds of sickness among the people.

Great crowds followed Him everywhere, and over all the countryside men were telling of His wonderful works.

The four friends He had called to be 'fishers of men' were always with their Master, while Philip and Nathanael had come from their homes to follow Him.

One day Jesus left a crowded house in Capernaum where He had healed a palsied man, and went to walk on the seashore.

There He saw a man named Levi Matthew sitting at the place of toll—a table by the landing stage at which travellers passing by had to pay the taxes levied by the Romans.

He was busy taking money, for he was a tax-collector—or publican.

Like many Galileans, Levi Matthew had two names—one Jewish, one Galilean. Levi was a strictly Jewish name, but it is by his second name of Matthew that this disciple is best known.

Old stories say that Matthew came from Nazareth, and knew Jesus. In Capernaum he would often see Him on the seashore.

But he never dreamed that the great Teacher would honour him by speaking to him—a publican.

A Jew who became a publican was despised by his fellow Jews. He worked for the hated Romans. Besides, many publicans were greedy. They overtaxed people and grew rich by cheating.

That day as Jesus drew near the place of toll, He stopped and, to Matthew's amazement, looked across at him.

He called ! Clearly His voice rang out ! " Follow Me. "

And Matthew arose, left everything, and followed Him.

Matthew was so thrilled—so full of joy because Jesus had called him, that he made a great feast in his house. He invited his fellow publicans and many others, and they all sat down with Jesus and His disciples.

The Scribes and Pharisees saw the happy crowd. They were shocked and angry.

" How is it that your Master is eating and drinking with publicans and sinners ? " they asked His disciples.

Jesus heard what they said and He answered them.

" They that are well do not need a doctor, but they that are sick. I came not to call the righteous, but sinners to repentance."

From that moment the Scribes and Pharisees, who scorned the poor and miserable, were the deadly enemies of the One Whose love and tenderness for all men put them to shame.

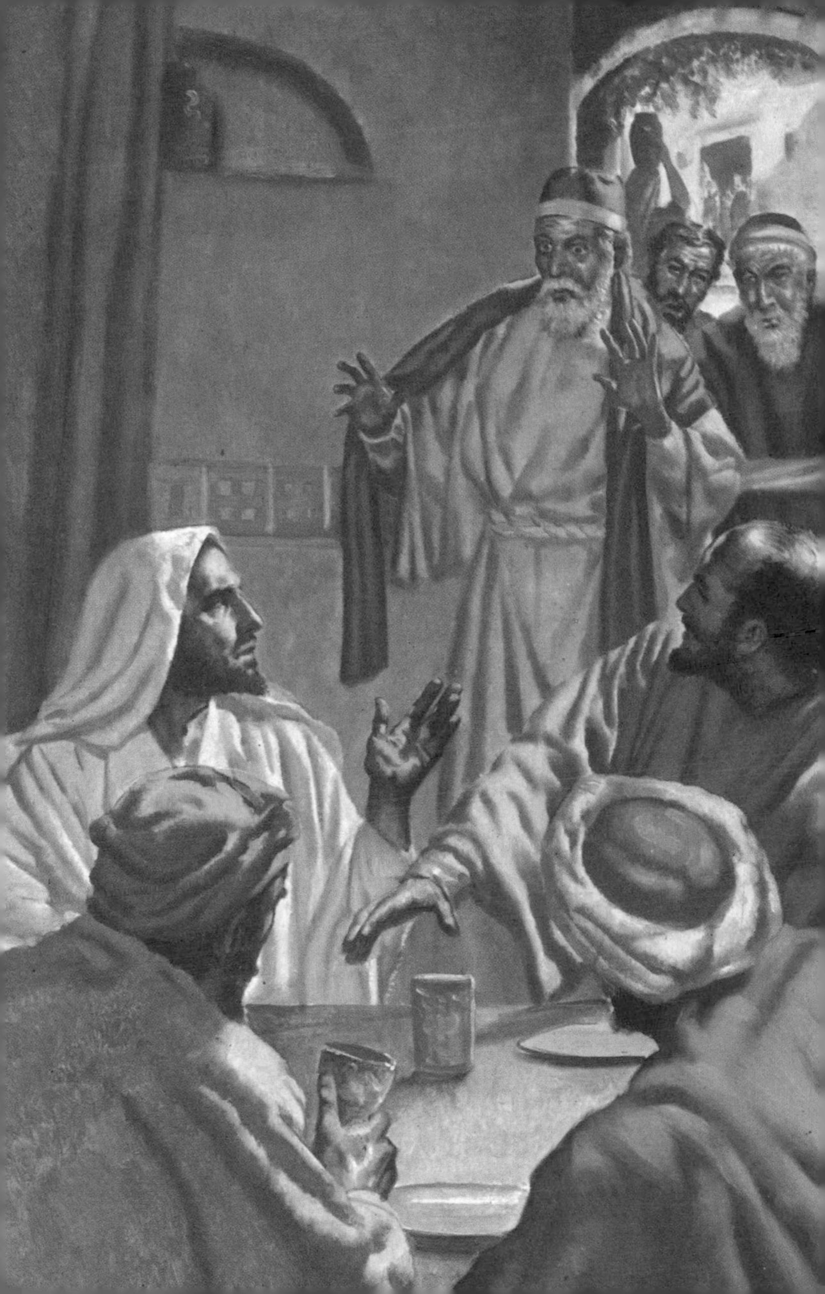

One evening Jesus went up alone into a mountain to pray. He knew that the Pharisees and the rulers of the Jews were plotting to kill Him.

So He meant to choose from the many disciples who now followed Him, a little group whom He could keep always very close to Himself. They should be taught and trained to be Apostles—' men sent forth ' in His Name to preach the Gospel.

All that night Jesus prayed, and when it was day He went back to His disciples. He chose twelve from among them, calling them by name.

Simon, whom He called Peter, and Andrew his brother.

James and John, the sons of Zebedee.

Philip and Nathanael Bartholomew, Matthew and Thomas, James, Simon, and Judas, the sons of Alphæus—and Judas Iscariot " which also betrayed Him."

Let us look at these twelve men who, at the call of Jesus, grouped themselves around Him on that day of long ago.

Some of them we know were already devoted followers of the Master—Simon Peter and Andrew, Philip and Nathanael, Matthew, and James and John, whom our Lord surnamed ' Boanerges, the sons of thunder', because of their quick, fiery tempers.

The others are new names in the Gospel story.

Thomas, called Didymus, ' a twin ', was a friend of Matthew. He got the name of ' The Doubter,' because he would not believe anything until he had proved it true.

He would not believe Christ had risen, until Jesus Himself stood before him with outstretched hands saying:

" See My hands, Thomas. Put your fingers into the print of the nails, and believe."

Only then did Thomas cry, " My Lord and my God."

James, Simon, and Judas were the sons of Alphæus or Cleophas, a brother of Joseph.

Simon the ' Cananæan ' or ' Zealot ', was one of a band of Galilean Jews who had a fierce love for their own country. Had they been strong enough, they would have plotted to destroy the hated power of Rome.

His brother Judas Lebbeus, surnamed Thaddaeus, loved his country as intensely as Simon. He longed to see the Jews freed from their conquerors, and looked anxiously for the coming of the promised Messiah.

James, the third brother, sometimes called James the Less to distinguish him from James the son of Zebedee, was as ardent a Jew as his brothers, and watched just as hopefully for the Saviour of Israel.

They did not understand that our Lord's kingdom was no earthly realm—but the kingdom of Heaven !

After the name of the last disciple which Jesus called that day, there is a sad note.

Judas Iscariot was not a Galilean. He came from Kerioth, a town in Judæa.

'Ish Kerioth'—Iscariot—means 'a man from Kerioth.'

This Judas seemed different from the other disciples. He loved money. He became treasurer for the Twelve, and kept the purse, and the more money he could get to put into it, the better he was pleased.

When Mary the sister of Lazarus poured costly ointment over the tired feet of Jesus, Judas Iscariot grumbled:

"Why was not this ointment sold, and the money given to the poor?"

He cared nothing for the poor; he was a thief, and took money from the purse for himself.

This was the man who betrayed his Master for thirty pieces of silver, but afterwards, how bitterly he repented!

The chosen twelve now went everywhere with their Master. James and John (the disciples whom Jesus loved), were nearest to our Lord, and Peter was always near them. Jesus often called these three apart from the rest. Peter, James and John were the only disciples He took with Him into the house when He raised the daughter of Jairus from the dead.

Andrew and Philip were very helpful. When our Lord fed the crowd of five thousand, it was Andrew who found the boy with the loaves and fishes, when he heard Jesus ask Philip what was to be done.

We owe a great debt to Matthew for, as he could write, he made many notes of the things Jesus said and did. It was from these notes that, long afterwards, the Gospel of St. Matthew was written.

But Jesus had not chosen the twelve to be hearers of the Word only.

One day He called them to Him and gave them power to heal all kinds of illness. Then He sent them away.

" Go and preach only to our own people," He said. " Talk to those who have forgotten God—the lost sheep of the house of Israel. Take nothing for your journey, and no money in your purse. When you enter a city, find a good man who will give you lodging, and stay there in his house. Your peace shall rest upon it."

So the disciples became Apostles, 'men sent forth' in the Name of Christ to preach and heal in Galilee, as one day, at their Lord's command, they would go forth in the power of the Spirit to preach the Gospel throughout the world.

Series 522